I0456381

I Use My Inside Voice.
I Do Not YELL!

By Suzanne T. Christian

TWORAVENS
B O O K S

Two Little Ravens
CHILDREN'S NON-FICTION BOOKS

Paperback Edition: 9781960320964
Hardcover Edition: 9781960320971
Digital Edition: 9781960320988

Published in the United States by Two Ravens Books LLC,
254 Chapman Rd, Ste 209, Newark DE 19702

'Expand the mind, free the imagination, one title at a time.'
www.tworavensbooks.com

Welcome to
"I Use My Inside Voice.
I Do Not Yell!"

This book is a treasure trove of easy-to-understand and engaging affirmations designed especially for young children. As you explore its pages together, your child will learn the importance of using their inside voice instead of yelling.

Each page features vibrant illustrations and positive affirmations that foster calm, respectful, and thoughtful interactions. By making this book a regular part of your reading routine, you can witness a gradual improvement in your toddler's behavior, as repetition is a proven teaching tool.

Prepare for a journey of emotional growth, peace, and lots of fun with your toddler!

Suzanne T. Christian

In the morning,
I wake up quietly.
I don't shout.

It makes the day
nice and calm!

On the school bus,
I chat quietly with my friends.
I do not yell.
It makes the ride fun for everyone.

At the library,
I whisper to my friends
like a quiet Ninja!

During storytime, I listen quietly.
Stories are more fun
when we hear every word.

During arts and crafts,
I share my ideas quietly.
Creativity needs calm!

I use my inside voice
when a grown-up is on the phone.
I do not yell.

At the doctor's office, I wait quietly.
It helps everyone feel better.

When I see a grown-up working,
I speak softly. I do not yell.
I use my inside voice.

During a video call, I talk quietly.
I don't shout.
It helps everyone listen!

At the museum, I speak gently.
Museums like whispering visitors.

At the zoo,
I point to the lions quietly.
Lions already roar!

At the supermarket, I ask for things nicely.
It makes shopping fun.

At the park, I play gently.
I can use my outside voice.
We have more fun
when we play nicely.

At the playground,
I wait my turn quietly.
Taking turns is fun!

When playing hide-and-seek,
I stay quiet and do not yell.
This keeps my hiding spot secret!

In the movie theater,
I giggle quietly.
Movies are better
when I do not yell.

When visiting grandparents, I talk quietly.
I don't shout. It keeps everyone happy!

At the restaurant, I speak softly.
This makes dinner time fun for everyone.

In the car, I use my inside voice. I do not yell.
It makes the car ride fun for everyone.

When my sibling is napping,
I use my inside voice.

Naps help us grow!

When we build a fort, I whisper.
It keeps our fort a secret!

At the dinner table, I use my inside voice.
Dinner is even more yummy with calm voices.

When it's bedtime,
I say goodnight quietly, without yelling.
This helps everyone sleep tight.

I use my
inside voice.
I do not yell.

The End!

My Amazing Toddler Behavioral Series

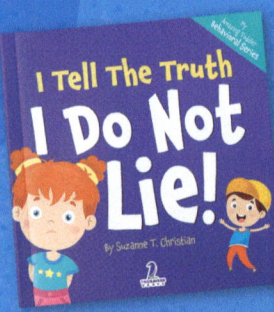
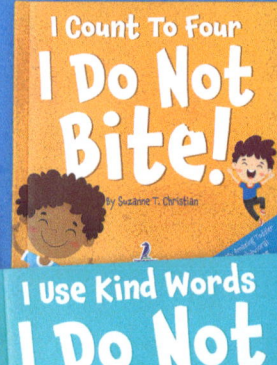
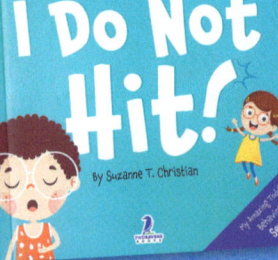
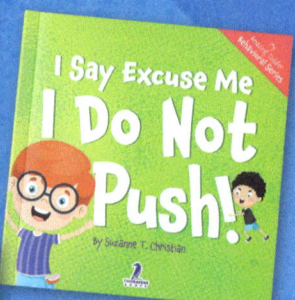
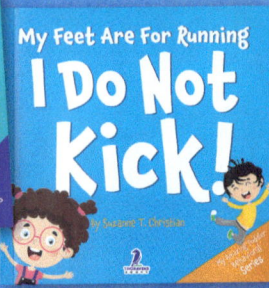

Check Out
Suzanne T. Christian's beloved series
'My Amazing Toddler Behavioral Series'.
Young readers are sure to enjoy!

Two Little Ravens
CHILDREN'S NON-FICTION BOOKS

Dear Amazing Reader,

Thank you for diving into **I Use My Inside Voice. I Do Not Yell!** with me. If this book touched your heart or made a difference for a young reader, I'd be grateful if you could share your thoughts in a review. Your feedback inspires my future work and helps others discover the magic within these pages.

I'd love to hear from you directly if you have suggestions or ideas for improving the book. Please feel free to reach out to me at **suzanne.christian@tworavensbooks.com.** Your voice counts, and I cherish it deeply.

With heartfelt gratitude,

Suzanne

www.ingramcontent.com/pod-product-compliance
Lightning Source LLC
Chambersburg PA
CBHW041600120626
46551CB00002B/270

9 7 8 1 9 6 0 3 2 0 9 6 4